YOU LUCKY DUCK!

Story and Pictures
by Emily Arnold McCully

A GOLDEN BOOK · NEW YORK
Western Publishing Company, Inc., Racine, Wisconsin 53404

Bruno and Sophie and their children, Edwin, Sarah, and Zaza, owned and operated the Farm Theater. After a wildly successful season, they closed for vacation while Bruno wrote an important new play.

Sophie had been too busy to explore the countryside, so she used the time to go sightseeing. She was often recognized, and everyone was friendly.

Edwin and Sarah practiced swordplay and
elocution.

And Zaza went to visit her new friend, Shirl. At
Shirl's house everyone paddled around a pond
and ate weeds.

It was a lot of fun at Shirl's. Everything her family did was ordinary. They had never heard of the Farm Theater, and Zaza didn't tell them. She was beginning to think her own family was a little weird.

When his play was finished, Bruno called a Production Meeting. "I've written the story of a great king and his three children," Bruno said.

"Bravo!" cried Edwin and Sarah.

"Where is Zaza?" asked Sophie.

Zaza was at Shirl's house, skipping rope. Shirl's mother was cooking dinner, and Shirl's father was mowing the lawn.

Zaza had forgotten all about the time. Then she remembered. "I have to go home," she said. "I have to work."

"Oh, stay!" Shirl cried. "I won't have anything to do!"

Zaza thought, "I wish *I* had nothing to do!"

At the Farm Theater everyone was already at work on the new play, *King Bear*.

"Zaza!" they cried when she came in. "Where have you been?"

"Having fun," said Zaza.

"Listen," Edwin told her, "Dad has written you a great part in this play."

"Ugh!" said Zaza. "I don't want to be in a play. It's embarrassing!"

The family stared at Zaza in disbelief. "You can't be serious!" they said.

"Why can't we just be normal?" Zaza asked.

Even Bruno was speechless. Finally Sophie said,
"Go to your room and think this over."
Zaza stomped off to her room.

When Zaza came down to dinner, she looked at her
plate and said, "Shirl's mother cooks *good* food."
She was sent back to her room.

Sophie went up to have a talk
with her. "We are troupers," she
said. "We have to pitch in
together."

"I don't want to work all the
time and be stared at," Zaza said.

Sophie was firm. "Our first
rehearsal is tomorrow. Be there!"
she said.

The next day they all read from Bruno's script. Zaza said her lines, but she kept wondering what Shirl was doing.

When Sophie showed Zaza her costume, Zaza
smiled in spite of herself.

When she and Edwin rehearsed their dueling scene,
she began to feel excited again, just as she always
used to.

Meanwhile, Shirl was so bored she wanted to scream. She decided to walk down the road until she found Zaza's house.

She heard voices coming from a barn. One of them sounded familiar.

Shirl poked her head into the barn.
Her mouth fell open when she realized what the bears were doing. "It's a play!" she said. "You're all in a play! Zaza! You lucky duck!

"It's so exciting!" Shirl said.
"Well, yes," Zaza said. "It's what we do here."
"Stick around," Bruno said to Shirl. "Maybe we'll find something for you to do, too."